written by
DIANE STORTZ

illustrated by
PATRICK GIROUARD

BARNABY MOUSE
DETECTIVE
and the MYSTERY of the
BIG BOOK

LITTLE DEER
B·O·O·K·S
PSALM 42:1

Standard Publishing
Cincinnati, Ohio

The Mouse family arrived
on Lovely Street on a Monday
afternoon. Mr. and Mrs. Mouse
had decided that the house
on the corner offered plenty
of room for their growing family.

Barnaby liked his new home right away.
The backyard was full of ivy vines and berry
bushes. "Perfect hiding places for an
undercover mouse like me," said Barnaby.

"You won't find many mysteries to solve around here," his father said. "The people in the house are kind. The children never fight—well, almost never."

But when night came,
Barnaby Mouse,
detective, launched
an investigation.

He scampered from
the windowsill to the
attic roof to the drain
pipe at the side of the
house.

He slid down the
drain pipe until he
came to a small
balcony.

Then he crept
toward an open window
and peered inside.

Books! Barnaby had never seen so many.
Big and little books, thick and thin books.
Books on shelves, and books on tables.
(None of the mice could read, but they
liked to look at the pictures.)

A man was reading
one of the books.
Barnaby scurried closer
for a better look.

The man's book was big. It was old and worn, and it didn't have pictures. *Why is he reading that old book?* wondered Barnaby. The other books in the room looked much more interesting.

It was a mystery! And Barnaby didn't have a clue. . . .

Until Tuesday, when he saw the book again!

He was carrying a piece of cheese up to the attic when he heard a small voice say, "Before you go to sleep, we have time for a story."

"Stories are found in books!" said Barnaby.

"This could be a clue!" He forgot about his cheese and followed the voice into the playroom.

A little girl was tucking her dolls into bed. The big book was beside her. When the dolls were snug, she opened the big book and pretended to read. Barnaby wasn't sure, but he thought the story was about a boy who shared his lunch. That reminded Barnaby of his cheese, and he hurried out the door.

On Wednesday, Barnaby saw
someone else reading the big book.
This time it was a woman.

After a while she bowed her head.
Was she sleeping? Barnaby didn't think so.
"This might be a clue!" he said.

On Thursday, the man and the woman had guests
in for supper. Company always meant extra crumbs
for the mice. But when the man opened the big book and read
to everyone before the meal began, Barnaby forgot about looking
for extra crumbs. "Something about that book is very important,"
said Barnaby. "I must keep looking for clues and solve this case!"

On Friday, Barnaby was in the playroom when the girl and her brother had a fight. "I told you not to touch my blocks!" the girl shouted. "Now I have to build my wall again. And I'm going to knock down your tower! You'll see how it feels!"

"It was an accident!" the boy shouted back. "Why do you have to build a dumb old wall, anyway?"

Barnaby ran under the toy chest to hide.

"**W**ell," said the girl, "I guess I forgive you. That's what it says to do in here." And she patted the big book.

"I'm sorry I said your wall was dumb," said the boy. "I'll help you build it again."

Barnaby had never ended a fight with his brothers and sisters that fast! Was this a clue?

Saturday was the boy's birthday. All of Barnaby's work on the mystery of the big book began to come together at the boy's party.

Barnaby could see that the boy's favorite gift was the one from his mother and father—a big book of his own! And this one had a picture inside, a picture of a man with very kind eyes. "Definitely an important clue!" said Barnaby.

The breakthrough in the case came on Sunday morning.

Barnaby saw the man and the woman and the boy and the girl getting ready to go out. The man was carrying the big book, and the boy was carrying his new one.

"I'll follow them," said Barnaby, "and maybe I will find out more about the big book." He hopped into the boy's pocket, and just in time!

Barnaby had never ridden in a car before. He was very glad when the car stopped in a parking lot and everyone got out.

"Look what I got for my birthday," said the boy to a roomful of children and a teacher.

"Your very own Bible!" said the teacher.

At last, Barnaby knew the name of the big book!
But the case wasn't solved yet. He still didn't know
what made the book so special.

Then the teacher said, "The Bible is like a letter from God to people everywhere. It tells us that God loves us, and that he sent Jesus to show us what that love is like. Reading our Bibles every day helps us learn about Jesus. And it can help us do the things God wants us to do."

So that was it! Now Barnaby understood why the big book was so important to the family that lived in the house on Lovely Street. The mystery of the big book was finally solved!

"Case closed," said Barnaby Mouse, detective, and he jumped back into the boy's pocket to be ready for the ride home.

The Standard Publishing Company, Cincinnati, Ohio
A division of Standex International Corporation
© 1994 by The Standard Publishing Company
All rights reserved. Printed in the United States of America
01 00 99 98 97 96 95 94   5 4 3 2 1
Library of Congress Catalog Card Number 93-14425
ISBN 0-7847-0004-4
Cataloging-in-Publication data available
Designed by Coleen Davis
Typography by Andy Rector